STO

FRIENDS
OF ACPL

3 1833 04795 3283

D1288462

· Major Bedhead ·

· Granny Gar

THE BIG COMFY COUCH™

Molly's Bad Hair Day

Written by **Cheryl Wagner**

Illustrated by **Richard Kolding**

ALEXANDRIA, VIRGINIA

Allen County Public Library
900 Webster Street
PO Box 2270
Fort Wayne, IN 46801-2270

One sunny morning, Loonette the clown woke up on her Big Comfy Couch, ready for a day of fun. "Morning, Molly," she called to her doll. "Time to wake up!"

Molly the doll was very quiet under Loonette's Dreamblanket.

"Want to play hopscotch?" Loonette asked. "Or even better, pirates? Want to, Molly?"

Loonette was always full of good ideas.

"Come out and play with me," sang Loonette, pulling the blanket off Molly's head.

But Loonette had a big surprise. Molly wasn't ready to play at all. Her hair was all tangly!

"Don't worry, Molly," Loonette said, searching under the cushions on the Big Comfy Couch. "I can fix that. Now, where are my comb and brush?"

But Molly did not want to get her tangly hair brushed or combed. She wiggled and squirmed and squirmed and wiggled.

Loonette understood why. "Don't be afraid, Molly," she told her doll. "I'll be gentle. But it's very important to brush or comb your hair every day. It's a way to be nice to your very own self—and to others who see you, too."

The little clown combed out her own curls.

"See? Don't I look better?

Now it's your turn."

But Molly did not want a turn. Ever. And especially not today.

What's a clown to do when her doll won't cooperate? A timeout seemed to be a good idea. Loonette decided to do her Clock Rug stretch.

Meanwhile, Molly had her own good idea.
She started to search under the cushions
on the Couch.

After her stretch, Loonette was full of energy, ready to get combing and brushing. She giggled when she found Molly back under the Dreamblanket.

"Come on, Molly," she said. "You can't hide from me. Time to fix that hair! I promise I'll be gentle."

But when Loonette pulled the blanket away . . .

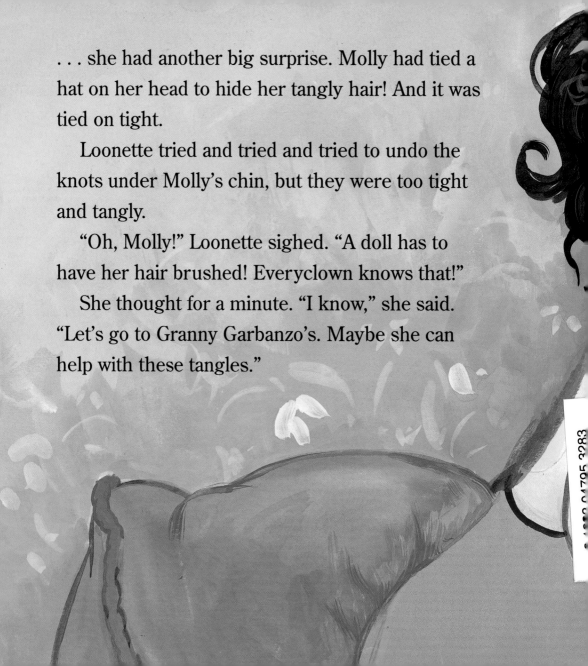

. . . she had another big surprise. Molly had tied a hat on her head to hide her tangly hair! And it was tied on tight.

Loonette tried and tried and tried to undo the knots under Molly's chin, but they were too tight and tangly.

"Oh, Molly!" Loonette sighed. "A doll has to have her hair brushed! Everyclown knows that!"

She thought for a minute. "I know," she said. "Let's go to Granny Garbanzo's. Maybe she can help with these tangles."

3 3283

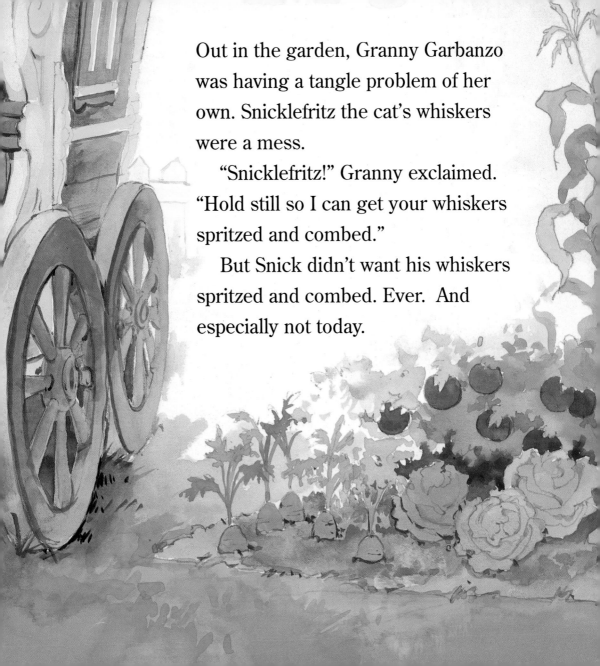

Out in the garden, Granny Garbanzo was having a tangle problem of her own. Snicklefritz the cat's whiskers were a mess.

"Snicklefritz!" Granny exclaimed. "Hold still so I can get your whiskers spritzed and combed."

But Snick didn't want his whiskers spritzed and combed. Ever. And especially not today.

"Can you help us, please, Granny?" asked Loonette. "Molly is having a bad hair day—and a bad hat day!"

"And I am having a bad CAT day!" Granny said. "But I'll try."

She tried and tried and tried, but she couldn't untie Molly's knots.

Loonette was getting worried. "Oh, I hope Molly doesn't have to wear this hat forever and ever," she said. "How could we play pirates—or princesses?"

But Granny knew what to do.

"Now, don't you worry, Loonetka," she said. "This Sunflower Whisker Spritz can untangle anything!"

Granny sprayed the tangled knots. Again she tried to untie them, very carefully, one by one. Presto! Molly's hat came off—and there was Molly's tangled hair.

"What a mess!" Granny exclaimed. "Looks like a plate of spaghetti."

Molly's hair looked so funny that Snicklefritz had a kittygiggle fit. Even Loonette had to smile.

"And just what are you laughing at, Mr. Snickerpuss?" asked Granny. "You look pretty funny yourself with those wild, woolly whiskers."

Now it was Molly's turn to giggle.

"You two are quite a pair: Miss Spaghetti Head and Mr. Noodley Nose," said Granny, holding up her mirror. Molly and Snick could see how funny they looked. Their tangles needed fixing fast.

Loonette had just the right idea. "I think it's time for the grand opening of Miss Loonette's Beauty Salon and Barber Shop for Cats and Dolls," she decided. "I'll be the hairdresser!"

"And I'll play some grand-opening music!" Granny said.

Granny played her concertina while Loonette very carefully, oh-so gently spritzed and combed Molly and Snick. They were very brave and sat very still. And it didn't hurt at all!

Soon the tangles were all gone. Doll and cat looked their very best.

"There!" said Loonette. "When you look your best, you feel your best."

Later, Molly wanted to have a turn at being hairdresser. Loonette the clown was very brave and sat very still. But when she got spritzed, she couldn't help giggling. It tickled!

"This wasn't such a bad hair day after all, Molly," she said. "Let's call it our glad hair day! Because looking nice makes you glad."

Molly nodded. Everydoll knew that.

Loonette gave Molly a little hug. "And I'm especially glad you're my doll."

And guess what? Molly was glad, too.